Disciples

Doctrine

This is a work of fiction. All religious teachings portrayed here are a product of the author's imagination and are used fictitiously. Any similarities to current or past religious teachings are merely coincidental.

DISCIPLES DOCTRINE

KILLER WORDS PUBLISHING
Copyright © by C. L. Conolly 2023
Cover by C. L. Conolly

ISBN - 978-0-9886876-6-0

C. L. Conolly
www.clconolly.com
clconolly@gmail.com
New Ulm, Texas

Printed in the United States of America

10 9 8 7 6 5 4 3 2 1

As God created everyone to be equal, all disciples shall be treated and compensated equally.

Azril

Azril began living alone in the woods when he was very young. He was the fifth of seven children and grew up on a farm. His father would get up before the sun every morning and go out to the barn to milk the cows. His oldest brothers would get up about an hour after his father and go out to help with the crops in the fields. As Azril got older, he was also given a job on the farm as well.

Azril enjoyed working on the farm. It gave him the sense of being closer to God. The beauty of the world around him filled him with peace.

His mother always held a bible study in the house with the family daily and she took the kids to church every Sunday. The church they went to constantly invoked the fear of a wrathful God, even though the Bible constantly told stories of a loving God.

His mother agreed with the pastor of the church. She would tell stories during their bible study about how God was a loving God, but would then contradict that with basically a story where He was intolerant of the way people lived their lives.

When Azril was thirteen, his parents

were fighting a lot. His mother wanted his father to join them at church on Sunday, but his Father never left the farm. After a few months of his mother insisting his father was going to hell, they decided to get a divorce.

His mother wanted to move to the city and be closer to the church, whereas his father cared more about the farm than he did about the church. He knew that taking care of God's creation was more important than worshiping him in a building.

Once the divorce was finalized, his mother moved into the city. Azril wanted to stay on the farm with his father, but his mother only allowed his two oldest siblings to stay on the farm with his dad because they were over the age of eighteen.

Azril decided he wanted to live on his own and take care of his own farm. He wrapped seeds for several different kinds of vegetables in aluminum foil and packed them into his bag before leaving home in the middle of the night. He walked for several days, as far away from his mother's new home as he possibly could, before he decided to set up a living space in a deep wooded area.

He didn't have a way to see if his mother was looking for him and any time he came into contact with another person they never let on that they knew who he was. Azril was sure that eventually he would be forgotten and no longer looked for, so after a couple of weeks of him living in the woods he planted his crop seeds and began cultivating.

He was able to hunt the wild animals for food and his crops were flourishing. Azril enjoyed living alone without having to answer to anyone, but he always made time for God. He would meditate daily and believed God was communicating with him.

His only companion was a stray dog that had approached him when he was fourteen. One day when Azril was preparing a squirrel for a meal, a very thin, timid dog emerged through the trees. The dog was so emaciated he wasn't sure what breed it was. The animal was so dirty and missing most of its fur, Azril thought the dog might have mange. At first, the dog wouldn't approach him. He would set up a plate of the animal's organs and place it out near a tree that was ten steps away from where Azril was sitting.

The dog would slowly approach the plate and as long as Azril didn't make any sudden movements, the dog would eat, then lay down. After a while, the dog would hesitantly approach him and that was when Azril realized the dog didn't have a collar or tags, so he named him Buddy. He took the dog down to the river and bathed him until Buddy started to heal and his fur began to grow back.

The more time they spent together, the more Buddy began trusting Azril and eventually would bring in small animals for Azril to prepare for the two of them to eat. Buddy started gaining weight and they were a team. Azril was finally able to tell that Buddy was a German shepherd.

When he was fifteen, Azril and Buddy explored away from their living area in order to find something to make for shelter. Azril had spent a couple of years being exposed to the elements and wanted to have shelter. He had started a make shift shelter made from tree branches, rocks, mud and a discarded hemp tarp he had found in a field.

Azril was content with living surrounded by the beauty of the physical land. Twice a day, Buddy would trot off into the woods to hunt, while Azril would take care of the physical land, or meditate with God.

By the time Azril was twenty, both him and Buddy had a system and they were satisfied with life. Azril was happy with having Buddy around, but he was feeling lonely. He had spent seven years with very minimal human contact and he was beginning to understand when God told him he needed to go out to find a connected partner.

Since it had been so long that he had actually held a conversation with another person, he wasn't comfortable with seeking someone out. He was communicating with God about Him possibly sending someone to him, but the more time that passed by, the less he felt as though he would ever get a connected partner.

"Hey Buddy, what's for lunch this afternoon?" Azril asked his dog.

Buddy ran off as Azril set up the fire and went through his crop selection. As he began preparing to skin the animal that his dog would bring back to him, Azril heard the crackling of leaves and sticks. The sound was coming from something larger than just his dog.

Azril not only used Buddy as his companion, but also as a protector from predatory animals. The sound became slower and louder as the being approached Azril's living area. He tucked himself into his shelter and peeked out through the opening from where he entered.

The sounds of the footsteps stopped and Buddy emerged from the trees with a rabbit clenched in his jaws. Azril waited, watching from his shelter as Buddy placed the rabbit down next to the fire, then looked back into the trees where he had emerged from. The dog whimpered and another person stepped out from behind a tree.

"Who the hell are you?" Azril said, as he popped out from his shelter.

"I'm sorry. I saw the dog and he seemed to want me to follow him, so I did. When I noticed the fire and tent I hid, not knowing if there was anyone here. I didn't mean to intrude," the uninvited person responded.

She was dirty and appeared to have been living outside without resources for several days. Her clothes were covered in dirt and there were leaves in her hair. Even through all the grime, Azril could tell that she was a beautiful woman and felt a warmth in his heart as though God sent her to him.

"That doesn't answer my question. Who are you?"

"My name is Omegra."

"Why are you here?"

"I just left my parent's home and began walking. I turned eighteen a couple of weeks ago and made the decision to move out. My mother told me that I wasn't allowed to leave until she said I could, so I just left and started walking. Last night I slept under a tree. When I woke up this morning, I packed my stuff up and continued walking. That's when I came across the dog."

"Where is your home?" Azril asked.

"I'm not even sure how far away from my parent's house I am," Omegra replied.

"You are welcome to join me here until you are ready to move on to wherever you are going."

"I guess I could. It's not like I'm in a hurry to get anywhere."

Azril nodded, then began preparing the meat for the three of them. He hung up the rabbit by its feet and sliced open its belly. He scooped out its organs and prepared them for Buddy. He skinned the rabbit, by stripping off its fur. Omegra took the fur and laid it over a bed of leaves, fur side down.

"What are you doing with that?" Azril asked.

"I'm setting it up to dry the flesh. Once it's dried, I can tan it, sew several of them together and use it as the covering for our shelter," Omegra answered.

"That's interesting. How would that work?"

"Since the skin is thick, it will help reinforce the hemp tarp that is already there. Also, we can cut a couple of windows, one on each side, through the hemp and use the animal fur as a cover over those windows during the rain."

"What does it need windows for?"

"It will help with airflow during the summer heat."

"I only sleep, or meditate in there. Otherwise I'm tilling the soil and taking care of the physical land."

"I'll leave it for now and we can revisit the idea later," Omegra said, sitting on the other side of the fire from Azril.

"We huh? Does that mean you want to stay here with me?" Azril asked her, as he cut up the rabbit meat.

"Maybe. I don't have anywhere else to go and wasn't going anywhere in particular when I left my parent's house," Omegra said, shrugging.

"I've lived here alone for the past seven years and it would be nice to have someone else to help cultivate the physical land," Azril told her, smiling.

Azril separated the meat from the rabbit into three portions. Two portions were cooked over the fire with some of the crops mixed in and the third portion was tossed into the fire and cremated.

"Why did you get rid of the third portion of meat? What about the dog?" Omegra asked.

"Buddy gets the organs. The other portion is a burnt offering given to God as an appreciation for everything He has provided for me," Azril told her.

"That's interesting. I didn't see you as a religious person."

"I'm not religious. I just know how to appreciate what God has provided. The animals for meat, the crops for nourishment and the beauty of the physical land. Giving a burnt offering to God and living your life in a way that is pleasing to God, will give you a place in the promised land."

"I can get with this. Tell me more."

"Sure, one thing first. Buddy, please go

down to the river and bring us back some water."

Azril held out a bucket, as Buddy approached and clenched the handle in his jaws, before he joined Omegra and sat around the fire. Buddy headed off to complete his task, as Azril told Omegra that he was a disciple of God and he could hear God speaking to him through meditation. He was told that everyone on the physical land was created equal and must work equally to keep the physical land just as beautiful as God had created.

Omegra

After a couple of months, Azril and Omegra had branched out from the small area that Azril had originally claimed as his land. He had set up his shelter in the middle of a circle of five trees. It was a perfect place to go mostly unnoticed by the wildlife.

There was enough space between the opening of his shelter and the trees for him to set up a fire to cook his meals, along with a makeshift chair. The chair was a large log Azril had carved a sizable notch out of, so he wouldn't have to sit on the ground.

When he had first planted the seeds he had brought with him just outside of the circle of trees, he didn't realize at his young age that the wild animals would feast on those crops. He had worked for weeks to get the green peppers, tomatoes, carrots and okra to emerge from the soil and become actual food that he could consume.

Just the smallest of buds were being sought out by rabbits, squirrels, deer, opossums and raccoons. He was forced to find a way to protect his crops from the wildlife. He had ventured away from his halidom, in search of something he could place around that area in order to deter the animals from consuming his crops.

He was able to find a discarded section of a chain link fence. It was a start, but he knew he would need more. Eventually, he built a wooden frame and was able to attach plastic to that frame and planted his crops inside his makeshift greenhouse. It was open at the top, in order for the crops to receive natural sunlight as well as nourishment from the rain.

Plastic sheeting was always flying around, as most people would just discard their garbage out into the physical land without a second thought. Azril always cleaned up the litter he found, in order to preserve the beauty of the world God had created.

The greenhouse worked for him and he was happy with what he had. However, Omegra brought in strawberries to grow along the chain link fence that was placed in the center of his greenhouse. She had also created a planter box for lettuce and cucumbers. Omegra wanted to help him with more animals that could give them extra nutrients, other than the wild rabbits and squirrels they had been consuming.

"I'm going to go out and bring back a few animals that God has created to provide us with other things to consume. Not just their meat, but the animals can produce sustenance for us daily. As long as you are okay with that," Omegra told him.

"Where are you going?" Azril asked.

"I know where I can procure some animals for us. I want to help," Omegra said.

"Are you sure it's safe for you to go alone? Maybe you should take Buddy with you, or I could go with you," Azril said.

"I'll be fine, I promise. Stay here and take care of the City of Disciples," Omegra said, pressing her lips against Azril's cheek, then turning and disappearing into the woods.

Azril took the time to go into the greenhouse and pluck any crops that were ready for consumption. He placed them into the container to be prepared with their meal.

As his mind began to wander and all he could think about was horrible actions against Omegra, to which she would never return, he sought out the solace of speaking with God. He climbed into his shelter and sat in the middle of the single room. In one corner, he had placed a foam mattress, that he had found discarded at the curb in front of someone's house, in order to sleep comfortably.

In the center of the room, he had placed a round rug in order to use for meditating in his way as he communicated with God. Azril found the rug on the main road. It was all rolled up and nicely tied as if it had fallen off of a vehicle as it traveled down the road.

Buddy laid next to him, up against his leg. As Azril listened to God tell him the proper way to live in order to be a loyal disciple, he wrote down everything he was told. He knew that God was using him as a vessel to spread the message of the disciples. Ever since Omegra had showed up, Azril was communicating with God more often. He knew it was due to Omegra being an outsider and she would need to learn everything about becoming a disciple in order to be converted.

Azril was comfortable with living as a disciple, but he needed guidance from God as to how to spread the message to others. He was informed to spread the message of God to the outsiders in order to recruit new disciples. God told Azril he was the leader of the disciples and it was up to him to spread the message.

"God of wisdom and leader of the promised land, please guide me as I do what I can to understand your teachings as you communicate through me on the physical land. Guide me to make the right decisions on the physical land, in order for me to meet you in the promised land. I want to be the best leader on the physical land in order to show the disciples the right way to you in the promised land.

"Guide the disciples into trusting that I, as the leader, am directing them on the correct path. Knowing that each day the disciples are looking to me, as the leader of the physical land, to guide them to the promised land. Fill their hearts, as well as mine, with trust that you have chosen the best leader of the physical land. I am a disciple of God and I will appease you in worship," Azril prayed.

After several hours, Omegra returned. She was leading a cow and a bull by a rope that was tied around their necks, along with a hen and a rooster that were enclosed in a metal cage. At first, Azril thought she was bringing animals in as meat, but realizing that she had thought to bring in two of each animal that were able to mate with each other, he knew she had brought them in to procreate in order to supply them with a sustainable farm.

"Where did you get these animals?" Azril asked.

"There is a field where they all run free. God has provided for us. The cow will give us milk to drink and the hen will lay eggs for us to eat," Omegra replied.

"How long would we need to wait before these animals begin providing for us?"

"Eggs will be plentiful, as long as we

provide the hen and rooster with the proper nutrition. As for the milk to be in constant supply, along with the potential of consuming beef, the cow would need to procreate with the bull regularly. We will also need to incubate some of the eggs in order to grow the chickens for meat and allow them to lay more eggs. It just means we would have to wait for them to begin producing more animals before we would benefit from the spoils."

"Are we still able to give an offering to God for supplying us with the animals?"

"If we have to give an offering just to have the animals in our possession before we are able to flourish the land with the animals, we won't be able to reap the spoils the animals are able to supply for us."

"I need to look for guidance from God. Please excuse me."

Azril returned to the shelter for God

communication meditation. Buddy joined him back in his position next to Azril, against his leg. He prayed to God for strength.

"God, give me the strength that I need to get through this difficult time. I need strength in order to trust that I, as the leader of the physical land, am following your teachings in order to make it into the promised land. Please, God, give me the strength that I need to know that I understand your message for me to translate your teachings to the disciples correctly. I am a disciple of God and I will appease you in worship."

Once he was given his answer, Azril slowly reemerged from the shelter. Omegra was preparing the crops from the container for a meal.

"What did God tell you?" Omegra asked.

"He said that as long as we are thanking him through the offering of the meal we are consuming, the animals are welcome to join us in the City of Disciples. We are also to be connected partners and procreate, in order to flourish the physical land. We need to spread his message to make sure that everyone knows the true message of God and not the lies found in the book that has been named the Holy Bible," Azril replied.

Connected Partners

"What is connected partners?" Omegra wanted to know.

Azril explained that God deemed him as the leader of the disciples and the leader must perform a connection ceremony with each couple living within the City of Disciples. The land Azril and Omegra were living on had been blessed by God and deemed the City of Disciples.

"A connection ceremony is what the outsiders call a wedding. Since a wedding has become a union between only a man and a woman, for the disciples it is a connection between two disciples. All disciples are created equal no matter who they decide to be connected with, hence connected partners rather than any other title," Azril commented.

During the connection ceremony, there must be at least two witnessing connected partners. Since they were the first connected partners in the City of Disciples, Buddy was to be their witness under God.

Once they are connected, they are to unite their connection with becoming one flesh with the intent of procreation to flourish the physical land with more disciples.

Disciples who are not connected partners are not to engage in the activities of becoming one flesh.

Since all disciples are equal within the City of Disciples, any two disciples may be connected in ceremony. As two disciples are connected partners on the physical land, they will be reunited in the promised land. Two disciples becoming connected partners are able to become one flesh without the intention of procreation.

If a disciple is without a connected partner by the time they reach their thirtieth year, they are to either offer themself to the leader, or request the leader to appoint a partner for them. A disciple offering themself to the leader must understand that requires living in harmony with the leader's connected partner. That is not with the intention of becoming one flesh with the leader. The disciple must recite the offering to the leader. If they are offering themself with the sole purpose of procreation, the offer will be rejected by the leader. The intention of offering themself to the leader is for pure companionship without the purpose of procreation, nor is it to become one flesh with the leader.

Any disciples who offer themselves to the leader, will also not be the connected partner of the leader. Each disciple is only allowed a single connected partner, but the leader is able to become a companion for any disciple to share their secrets with.

Each disciple who is able to give birth to a child, must be willing to incubate that child and take care of that child for no less than twenty one years. If the disciple did not choose for the seed to take hold, nor are they ready to take the responsibility of the child, it is at the discretion of the disciple as to the decision of their own body.

Life begins at first breath and before then, the disciple who is breathing is of the concern of God. As God created everyone as equals, everyone has the right to choose what happens with their own bodies.

No governing organization has the right to control the disciples with anything other than God's message from the Disciples Doctrine. As the government believes they are protecting their citizens with their laws, the disciples within the City of Disciples are under the laws of God. God is looking to the best interest of His disciples, whereas the government is only looking to the best interest of control over their citizens.

When two disciples request to become connected partners, they must both agree on the partnership. Separation between connected partners on the physical land, is only allowed if the leader agrees to the separation after both of the connected partners have stated their reasons for the separation.

If a connected partner of a disciple is shunned from the physical land, God will shun them from the promised land. The disciple left in the City of Disciples has options in how they spend time on the physical land.

While in the City of Disciples, the connected partner of the shunned disciple may offer themself to the leader, or decide to stay single if they have children. If there are no children, they are able to request a new connected partner.

After a disciple's twenty first year, they are able to seek out a mate with the intention as a connected partner. All young disciples are given the opportunity to spend time among the outsiders. They are to share the message of the Disciples Doctrine with the outsiders and convert as many as they can.

If within that time they find an outsider they would like as a connected partner, they have the option to remain with the outsiders, or they can bring their potentially connected partner into the City of Disciples to be converted. If they remain within the outsiders, they then have the potential of being shunned, as well as their potential connected partner being shunned. If they are able to convert the outsider and return to the City of Disciples, they will find favor with God.

"What is the Disciples Doctrine?" Omegra asked.

"I have been writing down everything God has told me and that is the Disciples Doctrine. Soon I will be converting it into a book and it will be issued to every disciple as they join us here within the City of Disciples," Azril explained.

Isolation and Shunning

Omegra was very interested in learning more about the disciples and becoming a connected partner with Azril, but she still had a few questions. "What is shunning?"

"There is a lot of information to process about shunning. God not only created the promised land for loyal disciples, but he has also created the underworld for those who not only don't follow the Disciples Doctrine, but also those who are shunned from the physical land as well as the promised land," Azril began.

He went on to tell Omegra that any disciple who comes into contact with an outsider is required to invite the outsider to worship with the disciples, as a way to convert them as a disciple. All disciples in a partnership with an outsider must convert the outsider as a disciple before the leader is able to perform the connection ceremony. When the outsider relinquishes their funds to the leader, they will be a temporary convert until they are washed clean of their previous life.

Since the outsiders have cages to hold those who were engaging in evil acts, the disciples would have similar cages for isolation. The isolation chambers were for anyone in the City of Disciples with evil intent. If a disciple goes against God, or the leader, they would be placed in isolation. If an outsider comes in the City of Disciples saying they want to learn about the disciples, when in actuality they are there under false pretenses, they are to be placed in isolation. As such, anyone sent to isolation will be there for a set period of time determined upon the action they committed. In that same context, each disciple in isolation would be required to read God's message as written in the Disciples Doctrine.

For any outsiders who are inside the City of Disciples that end up in isolation, they are required to participate in personal worship sessions with the leader of the disciples. The leader will determine as to whether or not the one in isolation has become a loyal follower of God as portrayed in the Disciples Doctrine and they are able to be released.

Children are to obey their parents as well as the other adult disciples. Children who are less than their fifteenth year, are to be isolated by their parents within their housing units. Children past their fifteenth year, but before their twenty first year, will spend seven days in isolation with personal worship sessions with the leader and they are to read and familiarize themselves with the Disciples Doctrine.

As a disciple after their twenty first year, they will be placed in isolation for a set period of time dependent upon the evil act they had committed.

Evil acts that require isolation include:

- Disrespect for God, or the leader;

- Treating any other disciple as though they are less than equal to themselves;

- Taking something away from another disciple, whether it be directly from their hands, or secretly taken from their housing unit;

- Reporting false information about an outsider, or another disciple;

- Taking another disciple's connected partner with the intent to mate;

- Taking more than one partner with the intent to mate;

- Placing hands on another disciple, or outsider with the intent to inflict harm;

- And any use of a weapon, or ones own hands to release another disciple, or outsider from the physical land.

Anyone inside the City of Disciples who commits any of the evil acts mentioned in the Disciples Doctrine, will be placed in isolation for a set period of time determined upon the action. Once their time has been completed, the isolated disciple, or outsider must receive one cut from each disciple affected by their actions. As for the disciple, or outsider who releases another from the physical land, after they receive their cuts, the leader must then shun them from the physical land, just as God will shun them from the promised land.

Any disciple, or outsider who is released from isolation and after they receive their cuts, they must agree to live in the City of Disciples. They must also follow God's message as written in the Disciples Doctrine. The leader will share this message with all disciples through the worship service. If they refuse, the leader must then shun them from the physical land, just as God will shun them from the promised land.

God had also instructed that the leader must shun any disciple who decides to defect from the City of Disciples. Also, any outsider who tries to convince any disciples to defect, shall be shunned. A shunning ceremony must be performed during the worship service, so the other disciples may witness the consequences.

For any outsider looking to become a disciple in order to escape their previous life, once they have been washed clean, they are required to shun all outsiders from their previous life, or convert their friends and family as disciples. After a disciple is placed in isolation for the fifth time, they must be washed clean again, or be shunned from the physical land, just as God will shun them from the promised land. If a child over their fifteenth year, but less than their twenty first year, has spent five times in isolation, their parents must then be shunned from the physical land and the child will be under the parental watch of the leader.

All disciples over their twenty first year are responsible for themselves and are subjected to more harsh punishment than a child prior to their twenty first year. For those disciples over their twenty first year, they are at the possibility of being shunned from the physical land, just as God will shun them from the promised land.

Anyone who wishes to live in the City of Disciples must be washed clean of their previous life. If the new disciple then decides to share the Disciples Doctrine with the outsiders from their previous life, it must be with the express intent for the outsider to be converted. If the outsider does not want to convert, the new disciple must shun those outsiders from the City of Disciples. If the new disciple is sharing the Disciples Doctrine with the outsiders from their previous life for the intent of malice, both the new disciple and the outsiders must be shunned.

"That is a lot to remember about shunning," Omegra told Azril.

"You don't have to remember it all. Everything I just told you is in the Disciples Doctrine. Also, you have been with me long enough. You could also join me for worship and learn more," Azril said.

"Can you tell me about this cleansing of the disciples?" Omegra asked.

Azril led Omegra into his shelter. She sat down with her legs crossed on the carpet in the center of the shelter, where Azril would meditate and talk to God, as he found his writings about God's cleanse.

God's Cleanse

Azril organized the notes he had taken from his sessions with God. He always felt a warming connection to the words from God. He was happy to finally have some-one to share those words with, as well as a new disciples and possible connected partner.

"When an outsider wants to convert as a disciple, they are to sell all of their possessions and relinquish all their funds from the physical land to the leader," He began explaining. "The outsider is then washed clean from their previous life with the intent to find favor with God. The leader is the only one who can perform all ceremonies within the City of Disciples."

"The leader is very important to the City of Disciples. I don't feel worthy to be in your presence," Omegra told him, looking down at the floor.

"I'm here to help you feel worthy. God has sent you to me to be the first converted disciple, as well as my connected partner," Azril explained, before continuing.

God's cleanse requires the disciple to be submerged into water as the leader recites the cleansing ceremony. All disciples witnessing the cleanse will then join in with the God's Cleanse prayer. After a moment of reflection from the cleansed disciple, they will then recite the evil acts that will send them to isolation and promise to God that they will not commit any of those evil acts, guaranteeing they are a disciple of God and will appease Him in worship.

Once an outsider has been washed clean, they are then required to live within favor of God. All children are to participate in God's cleanse after their fifth year, when they are able to memorize and recite the evil acts. The child must be able to articulate and understand the repercussions of their actions. Only a disciple who is able to verbalize their devotion to God, understand isolation and what happens if they commit an evil act, is able to be washed clean of their previous life.

Any children who are non-verbal, or an

outsider who is non-verbal that would like to convert, they will be able to live in the City of Disciples, but due to the fact that they are unable to share the message from the Disciples Doctrine, they will spend the entirety of their lives in the light blue uniform. It is only to signify that they are to stay within the confines of the City of Disciples.

Generally, children within their first five years are testing everyone around them and learning what they can and cannot do. After their fifth year, children have basically figured out how they want others to perceive them and are more willing to be complacent and obedient. Children are born innocent. They learn evil from the world around them.

"If all disciples have to go through God's Cleanse, who performs the ceremony for the leader, if the leader is the only one who can perform the ceremony?" Omegra asked.

"I have already been through God's Cleanse. I went down to the river and submerged myself to my neck, then meditated in order to communicate with God. He told me everything I had to do and say, then I dunked my head, had a moment of reflection and recited the evil acts. God split the clouds in the sky and the glow of the sun peeked out, blessing me as the leader of the disciples. I went back to my shelter and wrote down everything he told me," Azril explained.

"So when do I get to go through God's Cleanse?" Omegra wondered.

"Once you have memorized all of the evil acts that will put you in isolation and you are able to recite them in order as listed in the Disciples Doctrine, we can go down to the river and take care of that.

Shortly after your cleanse, we can then be connected partners," Azril told her.

"I would love to join you as a disciple here in the City of Disciples and convert the outsiders as disciples as well as procreate and birth new disciples. Anything that is pleasing to God, I will follow you in worship," Omegra said, as she maneuvered her feet under herself and knelt down in front of Azril.

The Mark of the Leader

Azril held his hand out to Omegra and assisted her to her feet. He held her hands and gazed into her eyes. He was looking for genuine love for God within her soul before he gave her a copy of the evil acts for her to memorize. She read them over one time before they stepped out of the shelter.

"As the leader, I need to mark myself to signify the leader of the disciples. God has given me the decision of what the mark of the leader will look like, but I need to create a brand to press against my skin as well as future leaders that are chosen must also be marked," Azril told Omegra.

Azril pulled a piece of paper from his pocket and showed it to Omegra. He had drawn what looked like a sunrise with an eye in the center. The eye in the sun signified God's watchful eye looking down upon the disciples within the physical land. Omegra held the drawing against her chest and a single tear rolled down her cheek.

"We need to get someone to create this brand. It's amazing," Omegra said.

"I could create the brand, but I need the materials," Azril told her.

"I will get you the materials. I know

where I can get the metal and welding machine."

"Where are you going to get it? Will any of the items be acquired in a way that would violate the evil acts?"

"Not at all. I promise."

Omegra set off to gather the items needed as Azril tended to the crops and the animals. He set up a fire and prepared to cook for the three of them living in the City of Disciples. Buddy ran in from the woods with a squirrel in his mouth. Azril prepped the animal and fed its organs to his dog. Just before the meat was ready for consumption, Omegra had returned.

She had a fireplace poker, a box of metal pieces and a propane torch. She placed all the items at Azril's feet, then sat down and waited for him to serve the food. Omegra was excited to learn more about the disciples.

"I know you said all the disciples are created equal, but is there a specific chain of command?" Omegra asked, as they ate.

"The leader has twelve disciples guard. Those twelve are to keep an eye on the other disciples and make sure they are living their lives in a way that is pleasing to God. There is also a chain of command within the City of Disciples. Each converted disciple begins at the bottom of the chain of command. When the disciples are able to convert more disciples, they are able to move up the chain. Only the disciples guard should directly address the leader. There are exceptions to this, but the disciples must first take their requests to the disciples guard," Azril told her.

"What about the leader's connected partner?"

"The leader's connected partner and their children are just as important as the leader. The disciples guard is also there to keep watch on the leader's children when the leader is dealing with situations within the City of Disciples."

The leader is to maintain order in the City of Disciples and deal with the finances in order to keep the City of Disciples running. They are also meant to lead the worship services and share the Disciples Doctrine with the disciples. The leader is the disciples guide through the physical land, in order to lead them into the promised land with God.

The Disciples

During the seven years that Azril had been meditating and communicating with God, he wanted to know why he had been chosen as the leader of the disciples. Why was he the one who was to lead the outsiders to convert as disciples. Even Omegra wanted to know the answer to these questions.

"God had informed me that up until the birth of Jesus, He had His loyal followers. There were still outsiders who committed evil acts, but He was able to control the evil and reassure His followers that He was always there," Azril explained.

"I was always told that Jesus was born to save everyone from their sins," Omegra replied.

"That was where the trouble first began. The outsiders believed that their savior was put here to take on the burden of all their evil acts and anything they did that wasn't pleasing to God would be forgiven, as long as they followed their savior," Azril disclosed.

Their savior was supposedly sent to the physical land, from the promised land, to be tortured and murdered in place of all the horrible acts committed by the outsiders. When the new testament was added to their Holy Bible, the outsiders then became more violent and would illicit fear in anyone who didn't believe what they believed.

God teaches, in the Disciples Doctrine, that everyone has been created as equals and should be treated as such. The Holy Bible was written in a way that states men are more important than women. It shows that women are to submit to men. The worst stories in that book are the ones that are translated as people with a different lifestyle are sinful and aren't following God.

In the Disciples Doctrine, everyone, no matter what lifestyle they live, is created equal. God created them to be who they are and as long as they don't commit any of the evil acts as outlined in the Disciples Doctrine, they are living their life pleasing to God. In the beginning of the Bible it reads,

'God created Adam and Eve'. Essentially yes, he created a man and a woman for the sole purpose of procreation in order to create more people to live on the physical land. That didn't mean he created everyone to follow the same lifestyle with the intention of procreation. Adam and Eve's first two children mentioned are Cain and Abel. So right after God create a man and a woman, He decided to create two more men. Could it have been that Cain wanted to become one flesh with the intent of procreation and Abel preferred to become one flesh with another without the intent of procreation? Cain wasn't living his life pleasing to God whereas Abel was living his life pleasing to God. Maybe Cain found out that Abel wasn't looking to procreate and decided to take it upon himself to commit the first hate crime.

Due to the Bible being translated in so

many different languages and translated with the intent to incite hate within those who don't agree with the way it's being translated, the outsiders have created their own narrative as to what God's message was in the Bible. The Disciples Doctrine is meant to dispel the negativity that has been spewed over thousands of years. Bringing in the outsiders to convert as disciples to live their lives equally pleasing to God, can change the world to a more peaceful place to live.

"So because you decided to isolate yourself from the outsiders and return to the original roots of God's creation, He chose you as the leader of the disciples?" Omegra asked.

"That's one reason. It's also because I have been receptive to the message God has given me. I'm sure I'm not the first person to communicate with God, but I may be the first to listen to God's message about the disciples and guarantee to live my life, as well as assure all disciples to live their lives, in a way that is pleasing to God," Azril told her.

Converting Outsiders

Azril used the propane torch to weld the metal pieces in a way to match the drawing of the mark of the leader. He welded the brand to the fireplace poker, then placed the brand end into the fire that was used for cooking. As the brand heated up, Omegra read the evil acts aloud in order to memorize them for her cleanse ceremony.

Once the brand was glowing hot, Azril held out his right arm with the palm of his hand facing up. Omegra stood, picked up the brand and placed the mark of the leader against the inside of Azril's forearm. As his skin sizzled under the hot metal, Azril bit his bottom lip and sucked in more air than necessary.

He placed his left hand under his right arm and slowly moved his arm around under the brand. He wanted to make sure the entire brand was marked on his arm. When he was sure the whole brand was on his arm, he gently pulled his arm away from the hot metal.

Omegra placed the brand down on the ground as Azril examined the brand of God's all seeing eye within the sunrise. Azril felt a burning, stinging sensation from his elbow to his wrist. As he gently blew over his open wound, a cool breeze blew over the area and assisted with soothing the throbbing pain over his forearm.

"You are going to need to wrap that up in order to keep it clean, so it doesn't get infected," Omegra told him, as she retrieved a piece of fabric from their shelter.

"It needs to be seen, in order to convert the outsiders as disciples. They need to know who their leader is," Azril told her.

"For now, it's just the two of us. How about you wrap it up until it's healed and you can tell me about the process of converting the outsiders as disciples," Omegra told him, as she cradled his wounded arm in one hand and draped the cloth over the brand with her other hand.

She wrapped the cloth around his forearm and tied it off to secure it. Azril winced as Omegra pulled the two ends tight.

"The disciples living within the City of

Disciples, are required to go out to the outsiders and share the message from the Disciples Doctrine and convert as many as they can," Azril said.

The best way for the disciples to share God's message from the Disciples Doctrine was to go to well populated areas and lure people in to hear the message. If you just shout at people, most will reject the message. God gave everyone freewill to decide for themselves, so allowing the outsiders to meet with the disciples in a group setting in order to hear the message shared from the Disciples Doctrine, could make them more receptive to hearing the message. That way, if the outsider decides they don't agree with the message, in a group setting, an outsider can leave without feeling uncomfortable.

After the outsider initially hears the message, they should be encouraged to approach any disciple within the group if they have any questions. Also, the disciples should have several copies of the Disciples Doctrine available for the outsiders to purchase if they would like to read through it on their own. Any outsider who purchases a copy of the Disciples Doctrine should be invited to a worship service in the City of Disciples.

At the end of the worship service, the leader is to request any outsiders to come forward if they would like to convert as a disciple. The outsiders who approach the leader are informed that they are to sell all of their possessions and relinquish all of their funds to the leader. Those funds are used to purchase items needed for the City of Disciples, as well as compensation to the disciples for their work inside the City of Disciples.

As more disciples are converted and

brought in to live in the City of Disciples, the small amount of crops that Azril and Omegra have, will need to be expanded. It will be necessary to have more food when there are more people requiring to be fed.

Once the crops within the City of Disciples are flourishing, the disciples will cultivate the crops to not only feed the disciples within the city, but also to sell in order to have a constant flow of funds for the disciples. All disciples are compensated equally in the City of Disciples. Disciples are assigned equal work as they will be paid equally. Disciples can also earn bonuses by recruiting outsiders with special skills as new disciples.

The chain of command is also determined by how many outsiders each disciple recruits. The leader is the top of the chain, with the twelve disciples guard directly under the leader. New disciples are to report to the disciple who recruited them. For each five outsiders recruited by one single disciple, the disciple will earn a bonus for bringing in new disciples. The more new disciples each disciple has reporting to them, will rank them up within the chain of command. Disciples at each rank are assigned a color, so they know who they are able to associate with.

The new disciples, before they have participated in God's Cleanse, will wear light blue. Those in light blue are not to leave the confines of the City of Disciples and they are to shadow the disciple who recruited them until they go through God's Cleanse. After God's Cleanse, they will wear dark blue. Those in dark blue are then assigned a housing unit and they are allowed to congregate with each other. They are to take their questions and concerns to a level one disciple.

A level one disciple has recruited at least five new disciples, but less than ten and they wear green. They are to help all disciples in both light blue and dark blue and only congregate with all level one disciples. Those wearing green are to take their questions and concerns to a level two disciple.

A level two disciple has recruited at least ten new disciples, but less than fifteen and they wear orange. They are to help all level one disciples and only congregate with all level two disciples. Those wearing orange are to take their questions and concerns to a level three disciple.

A level three disciple has recruited at least fifteen new disciples, but less than twenty and they wear brown. They are to help all level two disciples and only congregate with all level three disciples. Those wearing brown are to take their questions and concerns to a level four disciple.

A level four disciple has recruited at least twenty new disciples and they wear red. It is the highest level of recruiting disciples. They are to help all level three disciples and only congregate with all level four disciples. Those wearing red are to take their questions and concerns to the disciples guard.

The disciples guard is chosen by the leader to be a go between with the disciples. The twelve disciples guard, as well as their connected partners, will be given a grey uniform. There are limited reasons for the leader to come into contact with each disciple.

Individual time with the disciples is when they have been brought in as potential new disciples, during God's cleansing ceremony, if they are placed in isolation and they require one on one worship time with the leader, and those wanting to become connected partners. For no other reason should a disciple approach, or try to speak to the leader. The leader and their connected partner will both wear a black uniform.

Only the disciples in light blue are able to speak to any level of disciple, but it must only be the one who recruited them, as they are to stay with their recruiting disciple until they have gone through God's Cleanse and are assigned their own housing unit. Each level of disciple has a different dining time for each meal. The disciples wearing dark blue will go out to recruit with a group of leveled up disciples. They are to walk through the group of outsiders as they are listening to the message and anyone who appears as though they are listening intently, the disciple is to pull them aside to help nudge them into recruiting.

If a disciple is out among the outsiders and decides they want that outsider to be their connected partner, the outsider must be recruited as a disciple first. The chain of command is still in place and the outsider must work up to the same level as the disciple before they are able to become connected partners. That is to ensure both disciples are dedicated to God and His message as told in the Disciples Doctrine.

Children that live within the City of Disciples are to wear yellow until their fifteenth year. If they have been through God's Cleanse, they will immediately be given a dark blue uniform. They are then able to go out with the recruiting disciples to recruit outsiders. After a disciple's twenty first year, they are able to seek out a mate with the intention as a connected partner.

All young disciples are given the opportunity to spend time among the outsiders.

They are to share the message of the Disciples Doctrine with the outsiders and convert as many as they can. If within that time they find an outsider they would like as a connected partner, they have the option to remain with the outsiders, or they can bring their potential connected partner into the City of Disciples to be converted.

If they remain within the outsiders, they then have the potential of being shunned, as well as their potential connected partner being shunned. If they are able to convert the outsider and return to the City of Disciples, they will find favor with God.

Physical Land and Promised Land

Omegra wanted to prove her loyalty to not only God, but also to Azril in order to stay in the City of Disciples. Any time she wasn't working with the crops, or the animals, she was reading and memorizing the evil acts in order to recite them during her

God's Cleanse ceremony. She found Azril amazing with God's light surrounding him.

"Tell me about the physical land and the promised land," Omegra said.

"When God created the physical land, He started with the plants and the animals on the land, before expanding to the animals of the seas and the air. Everything you see around you was created by God. He wanted to share the beauty of what He created with the creation of us. We are to take care of God's creation and keep it just as beautiful as He intended," Azril began.

God spent five days creating the beauty on the physical land. On the sixth day, He created people - in His own image - in order to take care of the physical land. God is all around. He is the plants. He is the animals. He isn't a physical being. God is metaphysical and omniscient. For six days, when the sun is high in the sky, disciples are required to care for the physical land. The seventh day is the day of admiration for God's creation and the disciples are to worship Him that day.

God wanted each person to have a set time on the physical land, so they could meet Him in the promised land. Once God feels a disciple had fulfilled their purpose on the physical land, He then calls them to the promised land. As the disciples worship God on the physical land as taught in the Disciples Doctrine, He is preparing a place for them in the promised land.

God had also created a place for those to go who didn't worship Him as taught in the Disciples Doctrine when they are released from the physical land. The promised land is only for the disciples who worship God as taught in the Disciples Doctrine, whereas those who don't, will go into the underworld when they are released from the physical land.

In the promised land, all disciples will hear the praises of God from soft, calming tones that radiate all throughout the promised land. Where on the physical land disciples can feel sadness, pain, worry and fear, in the promised land disciples will only feel love, happiness, euphoria and solace. All disciples who have been released into the promised land, become a watcher of the disciples still on the physical land.

Disciples who worship God on the physical land as taught in the Disciples Doctrine, will be awarded a watcher from the promised land. The watchers are to keep the disciples safe from harm and are to assist them in making decisions that are pleasing to God. Former leaders who were released into the promised land are assigned to be the watchers for the next generation of leaders.

When a disciple is chosen to join God in the promised land and they become a watcher, that disciple will have the ability to return to the physical land as a mission to recruit outsiders. The returning disciple will have all knowledge of the Disciples Doctrine and will be born into an outsider family and begin preaching God's message as taught in the Disciples Doctrine by their fifth year.

Due to God giving everyone a set amount of time on the physical land, He created illness and disease to plague anyone on the physical land. No one would be exempt from the possibility of illness or disease. This was God's way for both the disciples and the outsiders to put their trust in Him, that He knows what He is doing is best. If He feels that one of the disciples is able to change the outlook of just one other disciple or outsider within a short period on the physical land, then that disciple will be released into the promised land within just a few years. Those who would benefit from more time on the physical land, will be given a longer life.

Anyone who denies God on the physical land, God will deny them entry into the promised land. God understood that He would not be able to get all of the outsiders to convert to the disciples, but He wanted as many as could be converted. He wanted the promised land to be full of everyone who worshiped Him as taught in the Disciples Doctrine. If an outsider were to make it into the City of Disciples and pose as a disciple for malicious intent, the outsider must be shunned from the physical land, just as God will shun them from the promised land.

The underworld is full of pain and torture. For those outsiders who feel the need to be horrible toward others during their time on the physical land, God will shun them from the promised land and they will be sent to the underworld. This includes the outsiders who claim to follow their book they are told is God's word, then turn around and their actions contradict what they claim.

In order for the disciples to live on the physical land in a way that is pleasing to God, all disciples must use the prayers in the Disciples Doctrine to ask God for assistance and strength. As God created everyone to be equal, all disciples shall be treated and compensated equally.

The New Leader

As the new leader of the disciples, Azril was required to fill the City of Disciples along side his connected partner. Knowing that Omegra must be cleansed before they are able to be connected, Azril wanted to make sure she was all in to join him as a disciple.

"I'm ready for the cleansing ceremony. How soon after God's Cleanse are we able to be connected?" Omegra asked.

"There is one thing that must happen before you are able to be cleansed," Azril said.

"I have done everything required. I have assisted you with taking care of the physical land, I memorized the evil acts in order to recite them after my cleanse and I want to be your connected partner," Omegra practically whined.

"For all new potential disciples in order to even begin living in the City of Disciples, they are required to sell all of their possessions and relinquish their funds to the leader. You have yet to relinquish your funds," Azril explained.

"I don't have anything. I left my parent's home only a couple of days before I stumbled upon Buddy hunting in the woods and he led me to you."

"Where did you get the animals and all the materials for the leader brand?"

"I went home and told my parents that I was trying to live on my own and that I needed a few animals in order to live sustainably. They were willing to allow me to take what I brought back here. The other items were also obtained from my parents as well. They didn't understand why I needed it, but I told them it was important."

"It doesn't sound like you committed any of the evil acts in a way to gain possession of the items, so we can go through with God's Cleanse. Follow me down to the river, where the sun shines down and kisses your skin. This is where the ceremony will take place."

Azril and Omegra walked down to the river where they got water for drinking and bathing. The sun was glowing in a singular area over the water. Azril stood at the bank of the river, as Omegra stripped off her clothing. Once she was naked, she approached Azril and knelt down in front of him. He placed his hand on her forehead and began reciting the God's Cleanse ceremony.

"We are joined together today for this disciple to wash away their old life and emerge into their new life as a Disciple of God. God's cleanse is meant to fill this disciple with righteous indignation to feel God enter their soul. Once they are cleansed, they are expected to live within favor of God. After the cleanse is completed, the disciple is guaranteed a place in the promised land with God."

Azril removed his hand from Omegra's forehead and reached down to assist her to her feet. As she stood, Omegra held his hand and he led her into the water. Azril stopped once the water was at his ankles, as Omegra continued into the water until it was waist deep. She turned around to face him. Azril lifted his hands, holding them above his head, palms toward the promised land.

Omegra submerged herself in the water, as Azril began reciting the God's Cleanse prayer. "I bring to you my God, this disciple into the family of God. They are ready to join us here in the City of Disciples and are cleansing their old life out, as well as accepting their new life with You in their heart. We thank you for the promised land where we are meant to go once we are released from the physical land. We are Disciples of God and we will appease You in worship."

Omegra stood in the waist deep water, shoved her hands through her wet hair to smooth it back out of her face. She took a deep breath and began reciting the evil acts that will get a disciple placed into the isolation chambers. She was able to recount each and every one of the evil acts in order.

Once she had completed the list she said, "We are Disciples of God and we will appease You in worship."

"Perfectly said. Please join me," Azril told her, holding his hand out to assist her out of the water.

Omegra stepped up onto the bank next to Azril and locked eyes with him. Without breaking eye contact, Azril asked her if she could promise God that she would never commit any evil acts for all eternity.

"I promise. I am a disciple of God and I will appease Him in worship," Omegra responded.

They held hands as they walked over to retrieve her clothes, then headed back to the City of Disciples. Azril sat by the fire, as Omegra entered their shelter to redress. When she reemerged, she stood behind him and placed her hands on Azril's shoulders.

"Do we need to convert some outsiders to disciples first, or are we allowed to become connected partners now?" Omegra asked.

Azril stood and turned to face her. "We have both learned about the Disciples Doctrine and participated in God's Cleanse. We are both on the same level now and God chose you to be my connected partner. It is time."

He whistled and Buddy came running out of the woods. The dog ran up and sat down right next to Azril. The leader pet him on his head, then began reciting the Connection Ceremony.

"Today, in the eyes of God and these

witnesses, we bring together these two disciples as connected partners. Within this union, these two shall spend all of eternity together. Here in the physical land they are connected, so God may reunite them in the promised land. As two disciples connect here in the physical land, this is a bond that shall never be broken. To ensure that these two have an unbreakable bond, if anyone here has any reason these two should not be connected, please raise your voice up to God and speak your truth."

"I think we can skip that part," Omegra said, giggling.

Azril smiled at her and continued, "love is love and is shared between two disciples. Connected partners come in all shapes and sizes and God has created everyone to have a connected partner. These two disciples have decided to share their lives together here in the physical land. Once God decides it is their time to be released into the promised land, they shall also be reunited there with God.

"Do you, Omegra, promise to keep close to your partner and share your secrets with only your partner, as long as you both remain connected here in the physical land?"

"Yes, absolutely yes," Omegra answered, then recited the vows for Azril. "Do you, Azril, promise to keep close to your partner and share your secrets with only your partner, as long as you both remain connected here in the physical land?"

"Yes I do," Azril said, before finishing the ceremony. "As we have both agreed, let's praise God for the newly connected partners. God, please watch over these partners as they connect their physical lives together, so that you may reunite them when they are released into the promised land. May their connection be loving and accepting just as you have taught us."

"We are Disciples of God and we will appease you in worship," the two recited together, before sealing their connection with a kiss.

City of Disciples

Azril and Omegra began preparing the land to bring in new disciples. They wanted to recruit people with special skills in order to do things for the disciples. The disciples would need someone who could make the uniforms, a cook, a doctor and several other specialists.

The leader and his connected partner gathered rocks of all sizes and piled them up as a border around a specific area of the physical land. It was only about knee high, with a gap for them to walk in and out of the City of Disciples. They decided that the disciples would build their own shelter. As more disciples would enter the city, there would be more people to help build the shelters as well as expand the wall.

"I think the best place to begin recruiting would be a college. College students are just starting their lives and are learning a specialty trade. Plus, we are close enough to their age that they would be willing to trust us and listen to God's message," Omegra suggested.

"That could also help with them bringing in their parents and possible siblings as disciples as well. We need to find someone with a van, so the disciples can go further than walking distance in order to convert new disciples," Azril said.

"Let's walk to the closest college and just sit and observe the students. Maybe we could sneak into a class and possibly befriend some of the students before sharing the message of the Disciples Doctrine with them."

"That sounds like a great idea. I could go into the religious studies class and start a scene in order to intrigue the students enough to come out of the class and ask me questions about the disciples. I could start my first worship service with those students and they could invite more people to those worship services in order to convert a lot of disciples."

Azril and Omegra had a plan they were ready to execute and they left Buddy in the City of Disciples as they walked through the woods and headed for the main road. They walked along the road for several hours before they came across a college campus. Hundreds of students were either heading to their classes, or congregating all through the property. The two connected partners walked up and sat down on an unoccupied bench and just listened to the conversations the students were having around them.

They sat for most of the day observing the people as they came and went. When the students thinned out and all retreated to their dorms, Azril and Omegra headed back to the City of Disciples.

They continued walking back and forth to the campus for over a week before Azril and Omegra were able to intermingle with the students. Azril found out where and when the religious studies class was held and decided both he and Omegra were going to just walk into the class.

The time had come for them to share God's message as taught in the Disciples Doctrine.

Prayers of
the Disciples

Morning Prayer - Because you have given it to me, God, I will begin this day. I thank you for watching over me during the night. I will do my best to follow my leader's teachings today in order to please you and in accordance with your guidance. Please dear God, watch over me as I go through this day and take care of me. I am a Disciple of God and I will appease you in worship.

Evening Prayer - At the end of this day, I thank you for all the guidance I have received from you. I hope I have made choices pleasing to you. I have listened to the leader you have chosen for me and can only do what is best for me. Please protect me through this night as I dream of your Promised Land. I am a Disciple of God and I will appease you in worship.

Before Meals - Before we receive these gifts you have provided for us, God, we thank you for the physical land and all the crops, flocks and herds that you have maintained for us in order to nourish our bodies. We are Disciples of God and we will appease you in worship.

After Meals - We give thanks to our God for the delicious meal we were able to partake in. We thank you for the promised land where we are meant to go once we are released from the physical land. We are Disciples of God and we will appease you in worship.

For Guidance - God of wisdom and leader of the promised land, please guide us as we do what we can to understand your teachings through our leader of the physical land. Guide us to make the right decisions in the physical land, in order for us to meet you in the promised land. We need the leader of the physical land to show us the way to you in the promised land. Guide us into trusting that the leader is directing us on the correct path. Know that each day we look to the leader of the physical land to guide us to the promised land. Fill our hearts with trust that you have chosen the best leader of the physical land. We are Disciples of God and we will appease you in worship.

For Health - God, give me health through my pain. Watch over me in the physical land and grant me relief from my sickness. If you are ready to receive me in the promised land, please take me quickly. I appreciate You for all that You have provided me with here in the physical land and I am ready to give it up for the promised land. If it is not my time to join you in the promised land, please give the medics here the knowledge to get me through. I am a Disciple of God and I will appease you in worship.

For Strength - God, give me the strength that I need to get through this difficult time. I need strength in order to trust that the leader of the physical land is guiding me through your message, as it is the way into the promised land. I need strength to follow your teachings in order to make it into the promised land. Some days I feel as though I am falling away, whereas other days I feel like I am following you. Please, God, give me the strength that I need to follow your teachings as told by the leader of the physical land. I am a Disciple of God and I will appease you in worship.

Forgiveness - God, please forgive me as I have strayed from your message. I have had thoughts of defection and need to be turned back to the leader of the physical land, so I may meet you in the promised land. I know that you can forgive me of this transgression and lead me back to the right path toward the leader of the physical land. Help me correct my defector ways and remind me of the joy I have waiting for me with you in the promised land. I am a Disciple of God and I will appease you in worship.

For Love - As I walk through this day that you have given me, I am but alone. I trust in your love for me, but help me find someone in the physical land to love as much. Show me the way to love others so they may love me back. I am patient and am willing to wait for you to bring them to me. I am ready to serve them with the gifts you have given me. I am a Disciple of God and I will appease you in worship.

In Times of Trouble - God, I have problems and pressures that are overwhelming me. My leader is teaching me to seek you when I am in troubling times. The outsiders are mocking your teachings and I am having trouble bringing them into the City of Disciples. Take away my guilt and failure and reassure me that this trouble is only temporary. Give me the joy that comes from learning about the promised land and know that my time in the physical land is limited. Renew my devotion for you and the knowledge that without you I would be lost. I am a Disciple of God and I will appease you in worship.

For Relationships - I bring to you my God, my worry and hope you are able to help me with my current relationship situation. Please wrap your loving arms around me and my partner. Fill us with love, joy, patience, and understanding for you and for each other. Bring me and my partner to the promised land in meditation, so we may seek your instruction. If we are meant to be together, please bring us back together. If we are meant to part, please show us the way. I am a Disciple of God and I will appease you in worship.

Connection Ceremony - God, please watch over these partners as they connect their physical lives together, so that you may reunite them when they are released into the promised land. May their connection be loving and accepting just as you have taught us. We are Disciples of God and we will appease you in worship.

Release Ceremony - God of wisdom and leader of the promised land, please lead this disciple into the promised land as they have been released from the physical land. Watch over the disciples still remaining in the physical land and give them understanding, as they also wait for their release into the promised land. Give their connected partner the strength to continue to follow you, as well as the understanding as to why their partner was chosen to join you in the promised land. We are Disciples of God and we will appease you in worship.

God's Cleanse - I bring to you my God, this disciple into the family of God. They are ready to join us here in the City of Disciples and are cleansing their old life out, as well as accepting their new life with You in their heart. We thank you for the promised land where we are meant to go once we are released from the physical land. We are Disciples of God and we will appease you in worship.

Shunning Ceremony - God of wisdom and leader of the promised land, we bring before you the shunning of a disciple who has gone against the City of Disciples and against You. Just as we have shunned them from the physical land, You will shun them from the promised land. Be with all disciples as we forget about the shunned disciple and continue to look toward You. We are Disciples of God and we will appease you in worship.

Ceremonies and Leader Offering

Connection Ceremony

Today, in the eyes of God and these witnesses, we bring together these two disciples as connected partners. Within this union, these two shall spend all of eternity together. Here in the physical land they are connected, so God may reunite them in the promised land. As two disciples connect here in the physical land, this is a bond that shall never be broken. To ensure that these two have an unbreakable bond, if anyone here has any reason these two should not be connected, please raise your voice up to God and speak your truth. -Pause for response-

Love is love and is shared between two disciples. Connected partners come in all shapes and sizes and God has created everyone to have a connected partner. These two disciples have decided to share their lives together here in the physical land. Once God decides it is their time to be released into the promised land, they shall also be reunited there with God.

Do you (name) promise to keep close to your partner and share your secrets with only your partner, as long as you both remain connected here in the physical land? -Pause for response- (repeat)

As they have both agreed, let's praise God for the newly connected partners. (connection prayer)

Release into the Promised Land

Today we are here as one of our disciples has been released into the promised land. As this disciple had allowed God into their heart, they will be welcomed into the promised land just as God has told us about.

- If the released disciple had a connected partner:
- -(still living) While their connected partner stays behind and waits for their release, or
- -(released previously) As they reunite with their connected partner, we worship God and await for our release day.

God will give us the strength to continue to follow Him as well as giving us the understanding as to why this disciple was chosen to leave the physical land to be released into the promised land.

If anyone has any memories of this disciple they would like to share, please feel free to come up here and let us know all the good memories you have.

-allow disciples to speak- (repeat until no one else stands)

As this disciple has been released from the physical land, into the promised land, let's praise God for the promise of immortality. (release prayer)

God's Cleanse

We are joined together today for this disciple to wash away their old life and emerge into their new life as a Disciple of God. God's cleanse is meant to fill this disciple with righteous indignation to feel God enter their soul. Once they are cleansed, they are expected to live within favor of God. After the cleanse is completed, the disciple is guaranteed a place in the promised land with God. Join with me in reciting the God's Cleanse prayer. (cleanse prayer)

Shunning Ceremony

We are gathered here to witness the shunning of this/these defector disciple(s) from the physical land, just as God will shun them from the promised land. They are guilty of - state offense - (i.e. defiance, engaging in connected activities with one who is not their connected partner, conspiring with an outsider, etc.). For each offense they have committed against the disciples, they will be bled of their wrong doings before being released from the physical land. If the shunned disciple has wronged any cleansed disciple, please step forward. If you wish, you may assist in the shunning. This/These disciple(s) are now to be shunned. (shunning prayer)

Offering to the Leader

As I stand before the great leader of the City of Disciples, I offer myself to you as a companion. I do not feel as though anyone is worthy to me as a connected partner. As the leader of the City of Disciples, it is to your discretion as to whether I am worthy. I am willing to be at your beck and call and do everything you ask of me. Shall I not succeed as a companion, I do hope that I am still worthy of being a disciple who is able to remain within the City of Disciples. Please great leader, take my offering and fill my heart with the love of God.

Also written by C. L. Conolly

<u>Single Titles</u>
Friendly Misfortunes
Killer Suburbia

<u>Affair Series</u>
Forbidden Affair
Family Affair
Fundamental Affair
Fruitful Affair

<u>Cult Series</u>
Disciples Doctrine
(Four more torturous novels
coming soon)

About the Author

C. L. Conolly has been writing stories since she was six years old. She is able to take true life crimes and twist the heinousness into a fear inducing story.

C. L. Conolly has always been intrigued by the reasons people commit such violent crimes. Disemboweling and dismemberment tend to be the go to torture in most of her books.

When she is not writing, she is spending time with her family and pets. She is married with one son, a cat, two dogs and two grandchildren.